The Lost Kingdom of Karnica

Richard Kennedy

Illustrated by
Uri Shulevitz

Sierra Club Books/Charles Scribner's Sons
San Francisco/New York

The Sierra Club, founded in 1892 by John Muir, has devoted itself to the study and protection of the nation's scenic and ecological resources—mountains, wetlands, woodlands, wild shores and rivers, deserts and plains. Its publications are part of the nonprofit effort the club carries on as a public trust. The Sierra Club has some fifty chapters coast to coast, in Canada, Hawaii, and Alaska. For information about how you may participate in its programs to enjoy and preserve wilderness and the quality of life, please address inquiries to Sierra Club, 530 Bush Street, San Francisco, California 94108.

Library of Congress Cataloging in Publication Data
Kennedy, Richard.
The lost kingdom of Karnica.
Summary: Life in the Kingdom of Karnica is never the same after Farmer Erd unearths a valuable red stone in his field.
[1. Conduct of life—Fiction]   I. Shulevitz, Uri.   II. Title.
PZ7.K385Lo [E]   78-32052   ISBN 0-684-16164-8
This book published simultaneously in the United States of America and in Canada—Copyright under the Berne Convention
1 3 5 7 9 11 13 15 17 19 ED/C 20 18 16 14 12 10 8 6 4 2

For Maria and Christopher

R.K.

To Beth who loves the Sierras

U.S.

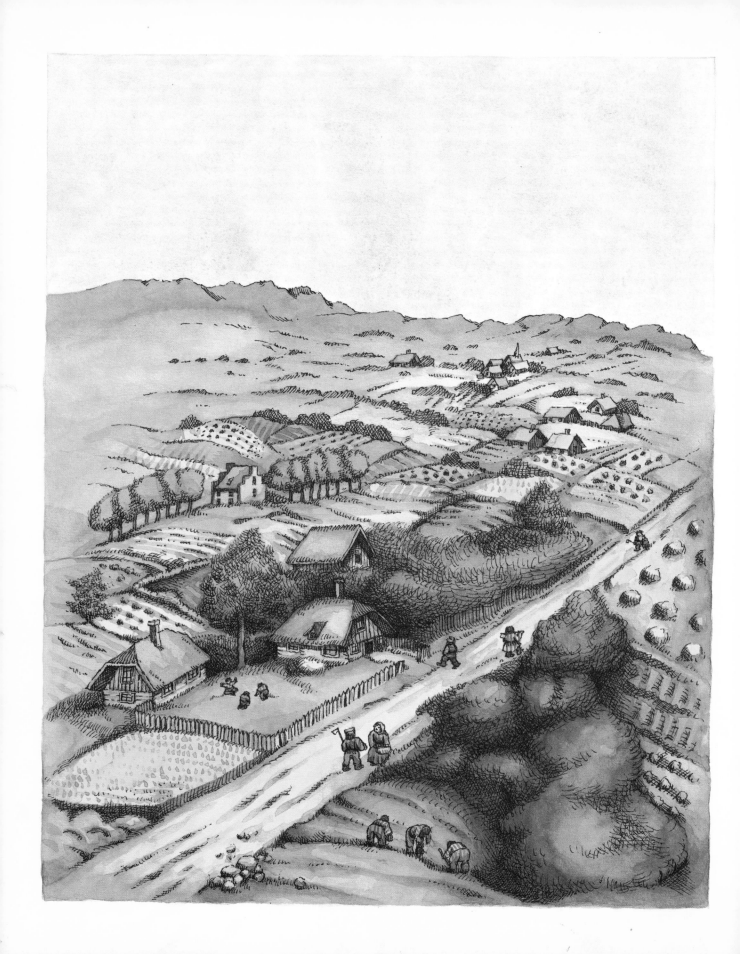

All things were not especially fine or wonderful in the Kingdom of Karnica before the stone was found, but the land was rich and yielding, and there was work and food for the people and a pleasant life for most. The king had never had the temptation to do anything really evil or the opportunity to do anything fatally foolish. And of course he had a wise man to give him good advice. But life got worse, and quickly, after the stone was found.

The story of how the stone was found was told many hundreds of times in those last days, and the manner of it was this: Farmer Erd was digging a well, a very deep well because of his ordinary bad luck, when he struck into the stone with his pick. He tried for half a day to dig around it, but with no luck, for the stone was enormous. Then he went home to sleep on the problem.

The next day he got neighbor Grum to come help him.
They took torches and tools to the bottom of the well.
Farmer Erd had the idea that they could split the stone with a
chisel and take it out in pieces. Grum held the chisel and Erd
hit it with a sledgehammer. "Whank! Whank! Whank!"

"Don't hit my muckle-muckle hand!" Grum cussed.

"I wouldn't hit your muckle-muckle hand," Erd said.

"Whank! Whank! Whank!"

A few chips jumped up from the stone, but it wouldn't
split. Erd wiped his brow. "What kind of muckle-muckle
stone *is* that?" he said.

"I'll be muckle-muckle if I know," said Grum.

"Let's give it a look," said Erd, taking up his flask of water. He poured some water on the stone and rubbed at it with his shirt-tail. Soon they could see in the fluttering torchlight that they were kneeling on a smooth red stone. Rainbows of light shone from it and washed like surf across the surface and settled back in golden-red pools of internal fire. It was obvious even to Erd and Grum that this was a precious stone, and it was bigger than a horse.

The men gasped and breathed out in awe and reverence, "Muckle-*muckle!*"

Erd and Grum then took an oath and swore on their mothers' graves to keep this find a secret, and they chipped off from the stone what they figured would be about a thousand dollars worth of precious gem stones.

That evening Farmer Erd had a dinner and a party for every relative of his he could find, and there were fifty-three of them at dinner, and more showed up later. Neighbor Grum went to town and bought drinks several times in several public places, and both men paid their costs with the flickering red gems.

Everyone knew about the stone in the well by ten o'clock the next morning. And so did the king.

"I'll have a look at that," said the king. He was taken to
the place upon his royal litter. He looked into the well, and
his royal goldsmith and royal jeweler went down into the
hole to make a close inspection. They came out of the hole
with the report that the stone was precious and of the highest
quality. The king told Erd and Grum that some king's men
would assist in digging up the stone. He was lifted up in his

litter, and he called out as the royal party left the place, "Dig it up! Jump to it!" And they jumped to it and began to dig up the stone right away.

The king's men worked all through the day while the news of the stone traveled around the kingdom. By dusk a thousand people had gathered to watch the working men who climbed in and out of the hole carrying dirt and water and tools. Washers and polishers were sent into the hole to make it shine like a jewel as it was being dug clear of the earth. The hole grew larger and a mound of dirt surrounded it. But the workers could not come to the edge of the stone, and at the end of the day the hole was forty feet across. Erd and Grum strutted about, telling their story and giving instructions that no one paid any attention to.

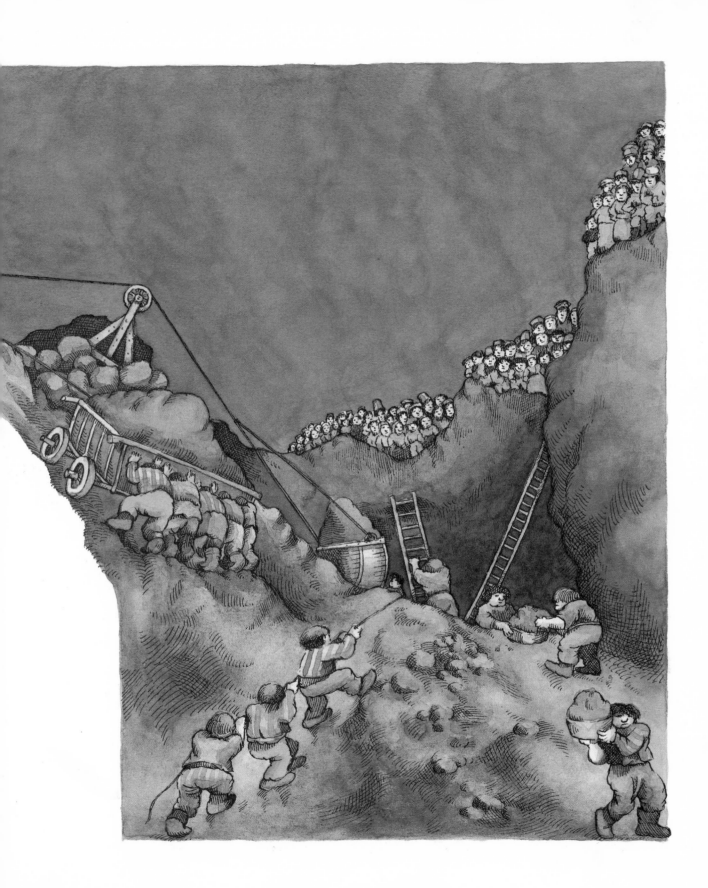

The king ordered on a night shift. That night he stood at a palace window and looked out across the darkened fair fields of Karnica to the mellow glow of torches where the stone lay. "Rich," he muttered, "rich!" A minister at his elbow leaned forward and said in his ear, "Indeed, Sire. We shall be the richest kingdom in the world...or elsewhere."

All night the king's men worked, and the next morning the day shift came on. By midday the hole was so large that the king ordered all those who had come to watch to go to their homes and return with picks, shovels and wheelbarrows, and they also went into the hole to work. The king himself moved to the site to give his personal attention to the labor. A banquet table was set up, and the king nibbled on grapes and dainties while attendants flocked about for his comfort's sake. They could hear him mutter under the linen

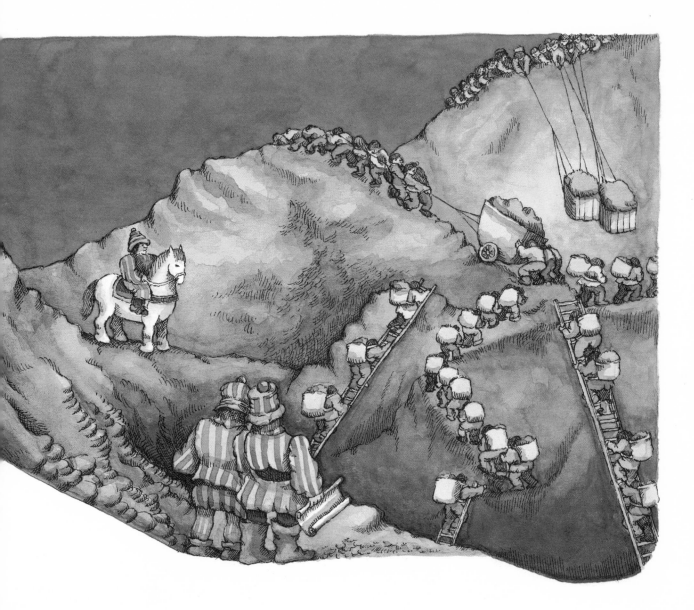

napkin he dabbed to his mouth, "Rich, rich!" Several times
the king was lifted in his chair and the banquet table moved
back to make room for the widening hole. The workers
worked all that day and all that night.

On the third day of digging, Farmer Erd's barn and house and fences were torn down as the hole reached out like a whirlpool. And then Neighbor Grum's farm was taken under, and the others. A circular hill of earth and debris grew up all about the hole, and there was no end yet to the great red stone.

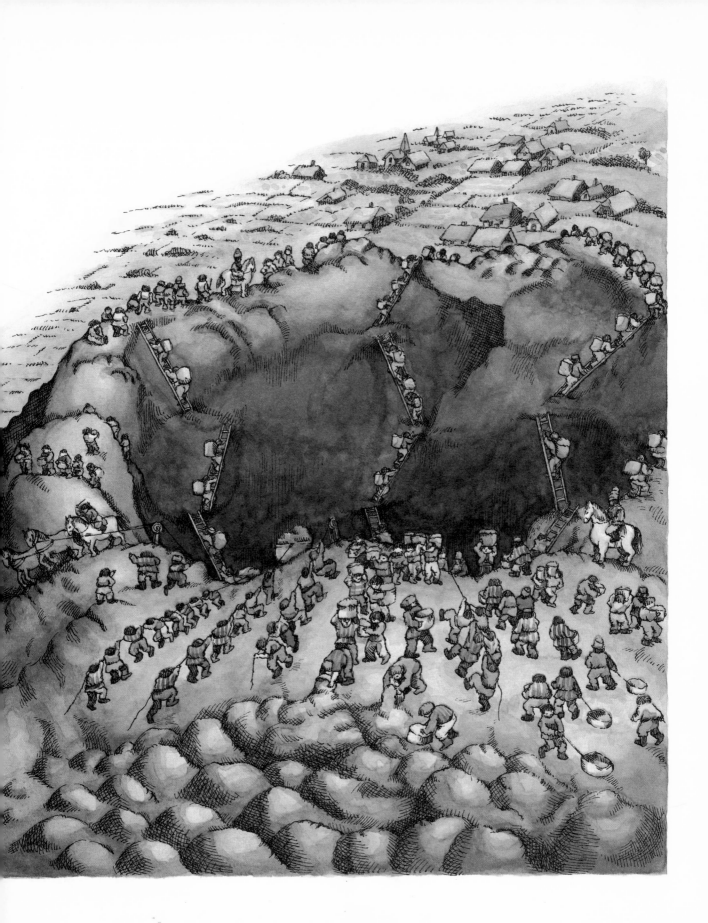

The wise man of the kingdom had not been idle all this while. He had been thinking, and wondering, and he had been studying his books. For long hours he had stood on the edge of the hole and gazed into the depths of the stone,

which seemed to him to burn with a living and moving fire. His thoughts went deep into this mystery, and at length he reached a conclusion.

Touching a knee before the king, and touching a hand to his breast, he said, "The stone is the heart of the kingdom."

The king paused between grapes, glanced at his minister, who smiled, and then the king said to the wise man, "Don't make me laugh."

In another day the royal treasury was half used up from hiring workers from neighboring kingdoms. The hole was now as big as sixty farms and four hundred fields, but there was no sign that the workers were coming to the edge of the stone. On the next day the royal treasury was completely used up, and the royal palace was torn down to make room for the

hole. The people of the kingdom and the workers lived in tents around the edge of the hole, and torches and campfires blazed at night around the great circle like the rim of a volcano. Inside the royal tent the king could be heard muttering, "Rich, rich!"

The wise man, sitting in his tent with a few books and a candle, sent word to the king asking permission to see him again. He was received in the king's tent. The minister was rolling up a map, and looked at the wise man sidelong and suspiciously.

The wise man dropped to a knee before the king. "The stone is the heart of the kingdom," he said. "And if we remove it, the kingdom will die."

The minister grunted, and the king said, "That's just a lot of muckle-muckle. Go away."

That was exactly the wise man's intention. He went about that night to several encampments, and in the glowing blood-red light reflected from the stone he spoke his wisdom that it should be passed about as a warning to all. For his trouble, he received only scoffing and sarcasm. On the following day the wise man bundled his few belongings together and walked to the ocean shore. There he found a man with a boat who promised to keep his books dry, and they sailed to another land.

Lakes were emptied, forests were cut down and rivers were turned to spill over the stone and wash it. Many more workers were hired, and great machines were invented that could dig faster than men, and everything was paid for with pieces of the stone. The hooves of horses were tied about with layers of soft leather, and messengers galloped across the gleaming surface of the stone carrying instructions and messages. At night, the thudding rhythm of the horses galloping across the stone sounded like a heartbeat to those who lay quietly on the earth and who listened.

The dirt piled up all around the edge of the stone
like a range of hills, and then the day came when the workers
had reached the borders of the neighboring kingdoms,
and yet the stone was solid in the earth. All the tents of
the workers were crowded onto the ocean shore of the
Kingdom of Karnica. The king could not dig into the
other kingdom's lands, and besides, part of the stone would
belong to them if he did so. He studied the situation care-
fully, and then gave his orders. "Yank it out! Yank the
muckle-muckle thing out!"

But it is much easier to decide to yank a stone out of the
ground than it is to yank it out. Because all the land of the
kingdom was dug up, the workers would have to pull at the
stone from the shore of the ocean, and from boats and ships
out in the sea. Therefore, many hundreds of boats and ships
were bought and built to do the work, and many fishermen
and sailors and crabbers were hired to man the flotilla. More

engineers were hired, and great winches were constructed on
the beach to haul at the stone.

The plan was this: long ropes were attached to the boats
and ships, and to the winches on the shore, and then fastened
to the stone in many inventive ways. It was hoped that all the
hundreds of boats and ships and winches would lift the great
red stone out of the earth on the outgoing tide and wind.

When the sun was on the horizon, the wind and tide swept out with a mighty lust, and the great red stone lifted from the earth and rolled over everyone on the beach and disappeared into the deeps, taking with it to the bottom of

the ocean every boat and ship. The waters of the ocean crashed into the empty hole and caused a storm which lasted for six days.

Then it was quiet and still. And there now ebbs a dark sea where the heart of the Kingdom of Karnica was torn from the breast of the earth.

That is the end of the story. The place is gone, and the people are gone. We shall not hear of them again. Surely it is a muckle-muckle shame, but it is the muckle-muckle truth.